Hooked by the BBC 3

Shady Business

Book 3 in the *Hooked by the BBC Series*

Amber Carden

CHAPTER ONE: The Unveiling 1

CHAPTER TWO: A Dangerous Proposition .. 10

CHAPTER THREE: Uninvited Guests 20

CHAPTER FOUR: The Indecent Proposal 30

CHAPTER FIVE: A Dangerous Choice 39

CHAPTER SIX: Bound and Blindfolded 48

CHAPTER SEVEN: Unfinished Business 56

CHAPTER ONE: The Unveiling

Sam and Mike faced each other on the front porch outside Andre's house, the bass from the music inside loud as the thumping in Mike's chest. Andre's proposal still hung in the air but that was the last thing on any of their minds. Mike was clearly nervous, his hand shaking despite the phone he held in it. Sam on the other hand, her patience was wearing thin and she was getting tired of waiting for an answer to the simple question she asked.

"I won't ask you again Mike, who was that on the phone? And I swear to God if you tell me it was work, I will end you." She demanded, the frustration evident in her voice.

Mike tried to think of the right thing to say, his mind was racing as he tried to come up with a plausible excuse for what he was doing. He had no idea how much she had heard but he knew that it was enough to incriminate him in her mind.

Sam looked into his eyes, looking for any hint of sincerity in them but she didn't find any. Instead, she could feel his hesitation and the silence between stretched until it became too uncomfortable to ignore.

Fed up with his silence, Sam threw her hands up, sighing loudly. "Fine, if you won't tell me then I'm done." She turned on her heel and headed towards the car.

"Wait, Sam where are you going?" Mike called out to her.

"Anywhere you're not!" Sam shouted at him, getting into the car and starting it. Mike panicked and raced towards the car, grabbing the keys out of the ignition.

"Give me back those keys, Mike. I don't want to be here anymore." Sam said, reaching out for the keys in Mike's hands.

"Please Sam, at least let me drive. I don't want you out on the streets in this state please." His tone was soft and the concern in it made Sam calm down. Rolling her eyes, she got out of the driver's seat and went round the car to the passenger side.

The ride home was uncomfortable to say the least, Sam looked out the window wondering just how deep Mike's deceit went. Mike could only grip the steering wheel as hard as he could, knowing that he would have no choice but to come clean otherwise Sam might do something drastic.

When they finally got home, Sam wasted no time. As soon as they were behind closed doors, she turned on her husband and demanded his attention once again. Her voice was shaky but it came out firm as she made her frustrations clear.

"Mike, I need the truth. Now. No more lies, no more half-truths, no dismissing this. What is going on with you? Please be honest with me." Sam paused as she considered another possibility. "Are you...are you sleeping with someone else?"

"What?! Oh my goodness, no. No! I'm not sleeping with anyone. It's nothing like that I promise you." Mike said, quick to reassure her.

"If it's not cheating then what the hell is going on here Mike? You've been so shady for a long time now, you're fielding calls whenever you're around me, you're taking secret calls. C'mon you have to admit that all of that looks a little suspicious."

Mike sighed, knowing his wife was right. "You're right, I understand how it looks suspicious, really I do. But the thing is, it's hard to be honest with you right now."

"Hard? What's hard about it? You were the one that made a big deal about us being honest with each other, so why are you taking your word back now?" Sam started to say, "What is so hard that you can't just tell me?"

"I'm involved in things Sam, things that you wouldn't understand. Things that could put you and I in danger, I can't just come out and tell you these things because it would seriously be putting you in danger."

"What is this? A gangster movie? You are a middle aged man Mike, in your forties. What could you possibly be involved in that is so hard to just come out and say? Honestly I don't know what to think here, I'm really disappointed. I thought I could trust you."

Mike exhaled deeply, Sam's words cutting deep into him. He didn't want to lose her trust, not over this. He hated to think that he had disappointed her in some way because of what he was doing but what was the guarantee that she wouldn't be disappointed if he told her what was happening.

The weight of his secret was heavy in his chest and he wanted nothing more than to be honest. He knew he had no choice but to come clean so he looked into his wife's eyes and began to speak.

"Sam, I never wanted you to know about this. In fact I never wanted you to ever find out like this." He paused and took another deep breath to steady himself. "I'm involved in something, something dangerous. It's something I don't want to drag you into, which is why I have kept it hidden from you all this time."

Sam's heart sank, what was he talking about? What has her husband gotten himself into? "W-what is it Mike, tell me. I'm sure we can figure it out together. Is it about your job?"

"It's not just a job...It has to do with something illegal..." Mike paused, unable to come clean fully.

"For goodness sake, Mike. Just spit it out already!" Sam shouted.

"Drugs okay? It's drugs, I'm dealing drugs. I make deliveries, running packages to discrete locations on behalf of this dealer."

Sam's breath catches in her throat and she tries to process everything her husband just said to her. "You're involved in...drugs?" she whispered, disbelief flashing across her face.

Mike nods, unable to meet her gaze. Sam took a moment to process what he just said to her "Mike, how could you get involved in something like this? Did you even think about what you were getting yourself into? Do you have any idea how dangerous that would be?"

"Look, I know that you have a lot of questions right now..." Mike started.

"I do have a lot of questions! Starting with 'what the hell were you thinking?!' How long has this been going on? Why would you get yourself into something like this? What if something had happened to you?" Sam said, throwing different questions at him.

Mike ran his hand over his face and walked over to a nearby chair to take a seat. He could barely stand, he was terrified. This was exactly what he wanted to avoid, he hadn't wanted her to know what was happening.

"Everything started over a year ago. Things were hard at the warehouse, I wasn't making enough trips and then this came along somehow. I only wanted to do it for a couple of months, make a little extra money on the side but then it got out of control. Before I knew it, I was way too deep and I couldn't leave."

"Is that what all those calls you've been ignoring are about? They are deliveries you're supposed to make on behalf of this drug boss?"

"Yes but not in the way you think. I stopped going out on their behalf and now I'm getting threats. That was what the call tonight was about, I think I'm in too deep and I don't know what to do."

"I can't believe this. You've been doing this for over a year? I've been by myself for months, waiting for you. Sometimes I spent the night all on my own and all that time you were dealing drugs like some...criminal?" Sam could feel her head spinning and she stumbled back till she bumped into a chair. Shaking, she took a seat as everything started to sink in. Her husband was a drug dealer, a 45 year old drug dealer.

"You have to quit, Mike." Sam said, her voice coming out much steady. "There's no future in that sort of thing, there's too much risk."

"It's not that easy, Sam. I just ignored a couple calls but look at the way I'm getting treated. Imagine what could happen if I left. They could hunt me down and do unspeakable things to me...I don't want that."

"So what do you want? You want to keep pushing drugs till you die? Look at you, you're not built like a criminal. I know it's hard but we have to figure out a way to get you out of this, you have to promise me you will try to leave this behind."

Mike nodded. "I promise Sam but I'm going to be honest, I'm scared."

"I know you are but you aren't alone anymore. I'm sure if we put our heads together, we can figure something out. I'm here for you now, everything will be okay."

CHAPTER TWO: A Dangerous Proposition

It had been a couple of days since Mike revealed that he was into the drug trade to his wife, Sam, and since then he was able to catch his breath. For a moment, it looked like things were finally getting calmer, that was until he got a call from none other than Tyrell.

Of course this wasn't the first time that Tyrell has reached out to Mike, but in Mike's experience he only got contacted by the head of the drug trade whenever things weren't going well. If he had to get a message to Mike, he usually did it using goons at his disposal. So for Tyrell to be calling him now, it meant that he was in serious trouble.

Mike's blood ran cold as he saw the name on the screen. Mike had been getting calls from some of Tyrell's men non-stop over the past few days, each time with more persistence. Mike had been avoiding those calls, hoping that he could buy some time to figure out how to get out of this mess but now it looked like he was out of time and he would have no choice but to face the music.

Tyrell wasn't a man to be kept waiting.

Reluctantly, Mike picked up the phone, his heart pounding in his chest. "Hello?"

"Don't fucking 'hello' me," Tyrell's voice came from the other end of the call, clearly irritated. "My men have been trying to reach you for days now and you've been icing them out. I don't like to get involved in petty shit like this so I'm going to give you the opportunity to explain yourself.

"Look, boss..."

"Ah ah, don't waste my time man. Get right to the point, why the fuck have you been ghosting?"

Mike squeezed his eyes shut as if that would protect him from Tyrell. "Look man, I've just been dealing with a couple things and I only wanted to take a few days..."

"A few days??? It's been weeks since you've been out on the road. And for what? You're dodging calls and you aren't making me any money, if you're not making me any money then you're dead to me." Tyrell's voice echoed through the phone, it was cold.

"It's just not a good time…" Mike started to say.

"I don't give a fuck about your time. You think I care what kind of time you're having? The only thing I care about is that you handle your business and make me money. Because of you, profits are low and you know how I feel about dwindling profits."

"I know…"

"So get back out there and do what you're supposed to do!" Tyrell shouted through the phone.

"But I can't." Mike croaked out.

"Why the fuck not?" Tyrell asked.

"That's what I need to talk to you about in person, I don't know if that would be possible at all."

There was a pause on the other end of the phone that put Mike on edge. Eventually Tyrell's voice came through the phone. "You better not be playing games with me Mike."

"No, no games," Mike said quickly. He got the sense that he was wearing Tyrell's patience thin. "Just let me say my piece and then I'll get out of your hair."

Tyrell went silent for a moment, then he finally said, "Fine, but if you're wasting my time then you're going to regret it."

"Thank you so much, where can I meet you?" Mike asked.

"I'll text you the details, now lose this number." That was the last thing Mike heard Tyrell say before he hung up. All he could do was look at the phone in his hand, his mind racing. He got the feeling that the conversation would be difficult, especially since Tyrell was the kind of man who didn't take too kindly to betrayal. But he had made Sam a promise and he was determined to keep it so he could earn her trust back.

Sam walked into the room, looking concerned. "I couldn't help but overhear your conversation. Who was that?" She asked, her voice soft.

"It was Tyrell, the leader of the drug trade. He doesn't call often but he's pretty pissed that I'm not out there making deliveries."

"So what did you guys talk about?"

"Nothing, I just asked for an meeting with him and I'm going to meet up with him soon."

Sam knew what that meant. Mike was going to plead his case in front of the boss himself. She knew that there was very little possibility Mike could get out of it, but she also knew that any more involvement in that life would lead to nothing but his downfall.

"Mike..." Sam started to say.

Mike nodded, almost like he knew what she wanted to say. "I'll be safe, don't worry about it."

It took a while but Tyrell texted Mike the details of their meetings like he said he would. Mike was to meet him at the nearest warehouse where they stored goods the next day, around noon.

Tyrell was waiting for Mike at the warehouse. As he made his way to the rendezvous point, all Mike could feel was nervousness. He had no idea what waited for him once he crossed the threshold into the warehouse. For all he knew, Tyrell could get rid of him as soon as he laid eyes on him.

The warehouse was quiet, there was no one in there and nothing apart from some stacks of wooden crates and metal containers that lined the walls. Tyrell emerged from the corner, then leaned against a stack of crates, his arms crossed across his chest and his eyes focused on Mike entirely.

Tyrell was younger than Mike, being only 39 but he carried himself with a confidence that made him appear much older. His skin was a deep, rich shade of brown and his head was completely shaved clean while he sported a goatee and mustache combos. He was wearing a black leather jacket underneath which was a plain white shirt. He looked alert like he was ready to stroke at any moment.

He was intimidating and that did nothing to help Mike's nervousness.

Mike stopped walking a few feet away from Tyrell. He couldn't read the expression on his face and that made it hard to tell what kind of mood he was in. "Thank you for meeting me, you look impressive as always." He said, trying to keep his voice steady.

Tyrell smirked and looked Mike up and down, "You look like shit, Mike," He said, ending his statement with a chuckle.

Mike didn't know how to respond, he waited until Tyrell finished laughing at his expense and then spoke up. "I'm sure you're wondering why I asked to meet you in person."

"I have to admit, I am curious but again, I don't like people wasting my time so get to the point Mike."

Okay, Mike thought, he wasn't in the mood for small talk. "I'm here to tell you that I want out."

The smirk on Tyrell's face vanished and it was replaced by a cold, annoyed look. "Out?" he repeated. "What do you mean, you want out?"

"I mean I'm done Mr. Tyrell." Mike said as firmly as he could. "I don't want to do this anymore. No more deals, no more deliveries, I have a family and I want that to be my focus right now."

Tyrell didn't say anything, the silence between them stretched for what felt like forever until he suddenly burst into laughter. "*I have a family and I want to focus on that,*" Tyrell mocked, "Man, you ain't the only one who's got a family. We all got families but we get our shit done and keep them out of it. So why are you coming to me with this weak ass excuse?"

Mike swallowed, "I just don't want to do this anymore, man. I've done so much for you already, I'm a middle aged man, I'm not about that life."

"Don't piss me off." Tyrell warned. "You think this is something that you can just walk away from? You're in deep, You fucking owe me and I don't let debts go that easily."

"Whatever it is I owe, I'll pay it-"

"With what money? You're in this business because you're broke as fuck." Tyrell said.

"What are you not getting? I'm done with the drugs." Mike said, standing his ground. His voice was firm, the most it had been since he walked in. But would it be enough to convince Tyrell to let him go?

Tyrell looked at him for a long time with his jaw clenched. He took in Mike's demeanor and he had to admit that he admired him for standing his ground.

"Let me make something clear to you, Mike. You cannot leave and you cannot buy your way out of this. If you think that then you're dumber than I thought you were. But I'm going to cut you a deal."

"Oh?"

"Yeah, I'll give you some time to think about it. Get your mind right, if you still insist on this 'I wanna leave' bs then I'll have no choice but to take drastic actions."

"How drastic?" Mike asked, swallowing.

"Let's hope you never find out." Tyrell said, turning away from Mike and walking back into the shadows.

Mike's heart started to race as he realized how bad the situation was. He couldn't believe how naïve he was, thinking he had a choice in this. Tyrell would never let him go that easily.

CHAPTER THREE:
Uninvited Guests

Sam was all by herself in the apartment, Mike had gone grocery shopping. Ever since he got back from Tyrell's, they had been laying low and keeping to themselves but they had no choice but to let Mike go out there and shop for food. Sam had never been this anxious before, her mind kept racing with possibilities. Her husband was basically a drug dealer and now he had gotten them into a terrible situation.

She was still pacing when she heard a loud, aggressive knock echo through the living room, causing her to jump. She had no idea who was at the door and why they would be hitting it so hard. She wasn't even expecting anybody.

Her heart pounded as she walked towards the door, the sound of her footsteps loud on the hardwood floor. The knock came again, more insistent this time. She hesitated as she reached for the doorknob, her hand trembling. She didn't know what was on the other side of that door but she had the feeling it couldn't be good.

Just as she was about to turn the door knob, the door burst open and three tall, hooded men trooped in. They were all big, muscular and dressed in dark clothes. The one in front, the biggest out of the three, had a hard look in his eyes.

"Where's Mike?" the biggest out of the three men demanded, his voice was low and menacing.

Sam swallowed. She knew instinctively that these were Tyrell's men, who else could they be?

"Where the fuck is Mike?!" The man demanded again, this time pointing a gun directly at Sam's head.

"I-I don't know," Sam stammered, trying not to show her fear at the gun pointed at her. "He's not here, he's not here right now."

"Bullshit," The guy said, turning to the other two men with him. "Search the place, he's got to be hiding somewhere."

The other two men nodded and went into the house to search for Mike, leaving Sam alone to who was no doubt the leader.

"Now, let me tell you something." The leader said, stepping closer, his presence intimidating. "If my men find your husband somewhere in this house, I'm gonna blow your brains out."

Sam shook her head, her voice trembling. "I swear, he's not here. I don't know where he is, he never tells me where he's going."

The leader's eyes narrowed as he studied her, he was clearly unconvinced. He yelled out to the other men, wanting to know their progress.

"Y'all find anything?!" he called out.

"Not yet boss!" One of them called out to him.

Sam could hear the sound of them breaking into rooms and ransacking them. She didn't know what to do, how to call them off or get them to leave. If they didn't find Mike, what were they going to do with her?"

The other two men came out from the inner rooms of the house and made their way to their leader.

"He's not here boss." One of them asked.

The leader cursed under his breath. "Do you think he knew we were coming?" He asked

"Nah, I doubt it. But what are we going to do?" Another masked man asked.

"We can't go back to boss man Tyrell empty handed, he's still waiting on his answer and he don't like to wait. So we have to wait till Mike comes around and jump his ass." The leader said, rationalizing their next plan of action.

Sam couldn't let that happen. She had to keep them away from Mike somehow. She looked directly at the leader, her mind racing with ideas on how to get them to leave the house before Mike gets back.

"Please," she begged, her voice a whisper, "Please don't hurt my husband. You can pretend like you never got here, I'll do anything."

The leader smirked, amused by her fear. He stepped closer, till his face was too close to hers. Sam could feel the heat radiating off him, the heady mix of sweat and cologne making its way to her nose. He reached it and tucked a loose strand of hair behind her ear.

"Anything?" he asked, dropping his voice to a whisper.

Sam nodded. She knew she was making a dangerous deal but she had no idea how else to get out of this situation. If she could do something to please these men and make them leave her husband alone she would do it. She didn't have much of a choice.

The leader's smirk turned into a cruel smile. "Good," he started to say, "then suck my dick."

Sam's eyes widened in shock at this proposal. She couldn't believe that he could be so bold as to suggest something like that.

"I can't do that." She protested.

"Bitch, you're the one that said anything." He said, standing up and unbuckling his pants. Sam and the other two men watched as he pulled out his cock, long and thick then stroked it to make it hard.

Sam looked over the penis that was in front of her. It was big, bigger than Jay's and Andre's and those two had pretty big ones too. If she had to guess, it would be around 9/10 inches. Just like him, it was intimidating as well.

"So what's it going to be?" The leader asked, still stroking his dick.

Sam watched as it got progressively harder. She swallowed, feeling a bit of arousal and anxiety about possibly putting that in her mouth. "I can't suck on that."

"Well you better fucking try, otherwise your husband's going to be on the other end of this," he nodded his head towards the gun in left hand.

Sam took a deep breath then crawled over to him, kneeling in front of his penis. She took it in her hands and it felt a little heavy. Sam took a deep breath before wetting her tongue, sticking out then trailing it all over the head.

"Oh, okay..." The leader sighed, holding on to Sam's head as she used her tongue to go up and down the shaft of his penis, wetting it thoroughly. She cupped her mouth around the head of the sick, swirling her tongue in circles around it whilst making a suction with her cheeks.

She wasn't ready to take it all in yet but there was a lot she could do before trying to shove it down her throat. She took her mouth of it, spat in her hand and then started stroking him, slowly, making twisting motions as her hand went up and down the shaft.

"Now that's what I'm talking about," The leader said, leaning his hips forward to be closer to Sam. She brought her mouth back to his dickhead, making swirling motion with her tongue while her hand went up and down his shaft.

The other two men are visibly aroused at this point and their erections we're straining against their pants. They wished in that moment that they had been the ones to take Sam up on her offer, the urge to cum in her pretty pink mouth was strong.

Sam worked the leader's penis until she felt she was comfortable taking a reasonable portion of it into her mouth. She trailed her tongue up and down his dick, wetting it to her satisfaction until finally she put her mouth to the dickhead and sucked it into her mouth, earning a long groan from the man in front of her.

"Yeah, that's right. Take this dick." He said, grabbing Sam's head with two of his hands and shoving his dick in and out of her mouth. Sam was taken aback by the sudden brute force from this man and tried her best not to gag as his dick went deeper and deeper into her mouth.

The man bobbed Sam's head up and down his dick, going deeper every time until he was hitting the back of her throat. He slowly pulled out of her mouth, his dick glistening with her saliva and smirked.

"Nah, I gotta tap that." He said, looking down at Sam. "Take off those pajamas."

"No," Sam said, shaking her head. She held her clothes closer to her body, as if to hide from his gaze.

"The fuck you mean no?" The leader said, his eyes narrowing in anger.

"The deal was I suck your dick and you leave my husband alone. If you're going to fuck then I'm going to need more from you." Sam said, trying not to let her fear show. She was taking a huge gamble, after all this man could just force her into doing what he wanted but she was going to take this chance.

"What more do you need?" He asked.

"Tell me how to contact Tyrell and you can do whatever you want to me." Sam said, her voice firm.

The other men burst into laughter but the leader stayed calm. He held his dick in his hands, stroking it as he was deep in thought. Eventually he smirked then said.

"You've got yourself a deal."

CHAPTER FOUR: The Indecent Proposal

Sam was elated that this man took up her offer. She took off her pajama top, slowly revealing the red lacy bra that was underneath. Carefully, she undid the clasps of her bra and let it fall to the ground.

"Damn, those tits are huge." The leader exclaimed, his eyes focused on Sam's heaving bosom. Sam slowly took off the rest of her pajamas until she was completely naked in front of the man. She crawled on all fours towards him, taking his dick into her mouth once again. She bobbed her head up and down the length that she could take in, creating suction by sucking her cheeks in.

The leader pushed her off him and she fell on her back onto the floor. He moved quickly, climbing on top of her and rubbing his dick against her vulva.

"Damn, I didn't think you'd be this wet. You a freak huh?" He said, before burying himself into her. "Oh shit." He said as he pushed himself deeper into her until he was completely up to the hilt in her.

"This bitch took all of that." One of the other men said in shock. He turned to his colleague to find that he had his dick out and was stroking it rapidly, his eyes completely on Sam and their leader.

The leader was different from Jay and Andre. Those men had been gentle, and tried to please her as best that they could. This man on the other hand, his strokes were as hard and rough as he was. He was not gentle by any means, pinning Sam down with his full weight, locking his arms around her and thrusting with a force that could only come from a virile young man.

It was uncomfortable for Sam but it was strangely arousing, especially when he grabbed unto her breasts and squeezed, swearing as he did so. Before she knew what was happening, the other two men came around. One of them knelt with his dick in his hand, shoving it into her mouth whilst the other one stood and watched the scene in front of him.

Sam had a full view of this other man's balls as he shoved his dick in and out of her mouth whilst their leader shoved himself in and out of her. "Holy shit," she heard the leader say, "this bitch bouta make me cum." he groaned.

He gave six more hard thrusts, moaning as he did so then pulled out of Sam rapidly and came all over her stomach. He groaned as rope after rope of cum shot out of his penis unto her skin. The other two men followed, the one with the balls in her face came full on in her mouth whilst the other one shot ropes of cum all over her boobs.

The three men stood up and started cleaning themselves up, leaving Sam in a mix of her juices and theirs. She stood up and watched them tuck their dicks back into their pants then putting their clothes back on.

"It's time for you to hold up your end of the bargain." Sam said, trying to put on a brave front.

"Oh yeah? And what bargain was that again?" The leader asked as he fastened his belt.

Sam's blood ran cold. Had she just given up her body for no reason? Had this man literally screwed her over?

"You're supposed to leave my husband alone and tell me how I can contact Tyrell." Sam said, raising her voice.

The three men looked at each other and smirked. The leader took a flip phone out of his jeans and threw it over at Sam who was still covered in cum. She caught the phone and looked it over, then looked up at the leader curiously.

"Call up boss man Tyrell on it. I can't say he'll be happy to hear from you but knock yourself out." The leader said as he and the men made their way towards the door that they had knocked down earlier.

"And what about my husband?" Sam called out to them.

"We'll leave him alone for now but Tyrell isn't done with him yet that's for sure." He said before leaving.

Sam lay on the living room floor, her body trembling with both exhaustion and shame. She didn't move for a long time, just started at the ceiling as she tried to process everything that just happened. She could still feel the roughness from the encounter, the way they had used her without a second thought. She didn't have time to dwell on what she experienced though, all she could was pick herself up. After all, she had done it for her husband.

She got up and made her way to the bathroom, placing the flip phone on a coffee table nearby. She needed to clean herself, maybe it would help her forget everything that just happened. She stepped into the shower and turned on the water, it was scalding hot but she didn't care.

She scrubbed her skin, until it was raw, as if that would scrub away everything that happened. She turned the water off and stepped out, wrapping herself in a towel. She went into the bedroom to dry off and thought about what she was going to say to Mike when he got back, how she would explain all of this to him.

She started drying her hair when she heard the front door creak. Her heater jumped into her throat as she quickly pulled on a bathrobe. Had those men come back, did they want to go back on the deal they made? Had they changed their minds so soon? Her mind raced as she stood by the bedroom door, waiting for any indication on who was at the front door.

"Sam?" Mike's voice echoed throughout the apartment. She could hear the panic and worry in his voice. She breathed a sigh of relief and walked out to meet him.

"Sam! Oh my goodness, are you okay? I saw the broken door, what happened? Is everything alright?" Mike said, dropping down everything in his hands and stretching his arms out to embrace his wife. She fell into his arms, squeezing her eyes so tears wouldn't fall. "Look at you, you're shaking. What happened?"

Mike looked down at her, his gaze soft. He was worried, he had no idea what happened here and he just hoped that Sam was okay.

Sam forced a smile but he could see that it didn't reach her eyes. "I'm fine, Mike. I'm okay, really."

Mike frowned, he was not convinced. "Sam, talk to me, clearly something happened here."

Sam looked away, unable to meet his gaze. "It was Tyrell's men," she admitted. "They came looking for you. They burst in and started demanding to know where you were. I was so confused, I didn't know what to do. "

Mike's face paled and he clenched his hands into fists. "What did they do? Did they hurt you? I swear if they hurt you, I'll kill Tyrell with these hands. "

Sam swallowed hard. She knew she couldn't lie to him. He deserved to know the truth. "They didn't hurt me, Mike," she said, her voice trembling. "But they were going to hurt you or even worse... unless I did something for them."

Mike's expression darkened, his eyes narrowing in anger. "What did they make you do?"

"I didn't want to do it but it was either that or let them do something to me and you. I told them I would do anything to keep you safe and then they made me…"

"Made you what, Sam?" Mike asked, his jaw clenched.

Sam forced herself to speak. "They made me sleep with them," she confessed, her voice cracking. "It was the only way to make them leave you alone. They left me this," she added, gesturing toward the flip phone on the table. "They said I could use it to reach Tyrell."

Mike staggered back, the color draining from his face as her words sank in. For a moment, he was too stunned to speak, his mind struggling to comprehend what she had done. When he finally found his voice, it came out hoarse and thick with emotion. "Sam… you didn't have to…"

"I had no choice," Sam interrupted, her voice coming out firm. "They were going to hurt you, Mike. I couldn't let that happen. What would you have me do?!"

Mike's anger faded, replaced by a deep sadness. He pulled Sam into his arms, holding her tightly. He didn't know what to say, didn't know how to make it better. After all this was his mess, he had brought this to their door. He had failed to protect her and that's why she did what she did.

He could only be grateful that his wife was willing to go so far for him.

He walked them over to their bedroom and Sam sat on the edge of their bed, her hand clenched in her laps. Mike stood across from her guilt weighing on him. Sam looked up at her husband and said, very firmly:

"I'm going to meet up with Tyrell."

CHAPTER FIVE: A Dangerous Choice

Mike snapped his head up, his eyes wide with shock, "What? No way Sam, Absolutely not. You're not going anywhere near that man."

Sam shook her head. "I have to, Mike. We can't keep living like this, with these men hanging over our heads. I need to do something to get us out of this mess."

"I already tried and that didn't work, what makes you think you can make any difference?" Mike asked, frustration seeping in.

"I at least have to try! It's not like things could get worse for us, we are currently living under the tyranny of a drug lord!"

Mike moved closer, his hands resting on her shoulders as he looked down at her with pleading eyes. "Sam, please. You've already done more than enough. You shouldn't have to suffer again because of my mistakes. I should be the one to deal with this."

Sam reached up, placing her hand over his. "I've already suffered, Mike," she said quietly. "But this isn't just about what I've been through. I can't live with that fear hanging over us."

Mike's grip tightened on her shoulders. "And you think going to Tyrell will solve anything? He's dangerous, Sam. There's no telling what he'll do."

"I know it's risky," Sam admitted. "But it's the only chance we have. I need to try and negotiate with him, to make him see that this needs to end. Maybe I can get him to let you go, to leave us both alone."

Mike's heart ached. He didn't want her to go, didn't want her anywhere near Tyrell or his men. But deep down, he knew they couldn't keep running. And he knew his wife would not give up till she got her way.

"Sam...," he began, "What if he doesn't agree? What if he wants something more from you?"

Sam took a deep breath. "Then I'll deal with it," she said firmly. "I have to do this, Mike. For both of us."

"Alright," he said quietly. "But please, be careful. I can't lose you, Sam."

Sam nodded, reaching up to cup his face in her hands. "I'll be careful," she promised.

Before she knew it, Sam was staring down at the flip phone those goons had given her. It was the only way to reach Tyrell and try to negotiate Mike's freedom. She wiped her palms on her jeans, took a deep breath, and picked up the phone. It felt cold in her hand as she flipped it open and dialed the only number on the phone that no doubt belonged to Tyrell.

The phone rang twice before it connected. There was a brief silence on the other end, followed by the deep, rough voice of Tyrell.

"Smith, you better have a damn good reason for calling me on this line," Tyrell growled, clearly mistaking her for one of his men. "You know better than to reach out like this. What the hell are you thinking?"

Sam swallowed hard, her voice shaking slightly as she interrupted him. "It's not Smith," she said quickly. "This is Sam. Mike's wife."

There was a brief pause, and when Tyrell spoke again, his tone was colder. "Mrs. Serrano herself, hmm? What are you doing with that phone? And where's Mike?"

Sam took a deep breath, gathering her courage. "Mike's not here. I'm the one who called. I need to talk to you."

"Talk to me about what? What the hell do you want?"

"I want to meet with you, in person. Somewhere private."

Tyrell snorted on the other end of the line, clearly amused. "And why would I agree to that? You think you can just waltz in and demand a meeting with me?"

"I'm not demanding," Sam replied, her voice firm. "I'm asking. I'm willing to negotiate."

Another pause, and then Tyrell sighed. "You've got guts, I'll give you that." he said, a hint of respect in his voice. "Alright, I'll meet with you. But this better be worth my time. If you're wasting it, I won't hesitate to take what I'm owed."

Sam's heart skipped a beat, but she forced herself to stay calm. "It'll be worth it," she promised. "Just tell me when and where."

"There's a warehouse on 34th and Lex. Be there at midnight. And don't even think about bringing anyone with you. This is between you and me."

"I understand," Sam replied, her voice steady. "I'll be there."

The rest of the day passed and soon it was midnight. Sam made her way out of her apartment in the dead of night while Mike was asleep and made her way to the warehouse Tyrell had set up. Her heart pounded in her chest as she approached the large, rusted metal door. She reached the door, and it creaked open as if it had been waiting for her.

The inside of the warehouse was dimly lit. Tyrell was waiting for her near the center of the warehouse, leaning casually against a stack of metal crates. He was dressed in a tailored suit, a weird choice of clothing for this time of night, Sam thought to herself. The look on his face was one of smug amusement and it made Sam uncomfortable.

"You're punctual. I like that," Tyrell said with a smirk. "It shows you're serious."

"I am," Sam replied. She stopped a few feet away from him. "Let's get straight to it. What will it take for you to leave Mike alone?"

Tyrell chuckled, a low, mocking sound. "Straight to the point, huh? I respect that. Look honey, your husband owes me a lot of money, and I don't see how you're going to change that. What exactly do you have to negotiate with?"

"I'm willing to buy his freedom," she said, "I'll do whatever it takes to get you to leave him alone. I don't care if I have to work or anything, just leave my husband alone. "

There was a lone pause as Tyrell pondered the woman in front of him. "I'm not the kind of man that gives second chances, Sam but I happen to know that you're willing to go the extra mile. My boys told me all about what happened back at your place."

Sam felt her cheeks flush with embarrassment. She hadn't expected Tyrell to know about what had transpired with his men, let alone bring it up so casually.

"What does that have to do with anything?" she demanded. "I did what I had to do to protect Mike. That's all that matters."

Tyrell pushed himself off the crates and took a step closer to her, "Oh, it has everything to do with this. You see, Sam, you've already shown me how far you're willing to go. You've proven you're desperate enough to do whatever it takes. That gives me all the leverage I need."

Sam's heart sank "What do you want from me, Tyrell?" she asked, her voice trembling slightly. "I'm here to negotiate Mike's freedom. Just tell me what it'll take."

Tyrell grinned. "It's simple," he said, "I'll let your husband go, but only if you agree to become my property for a while."

Sam's eyes widened in shock, her breath catching in her throat. She couldn't believe what she was hearing. "Your... property?" she echoed.

Tyrell nodded. "That's right. You'll belong to me. You'll do whatever I say, whenever I say it. And in return, I'll make sure Mike walks away from all this unscathed."

"You said you were willing to do whatever it took. You made a big show about it, coming here and making demands in my territory. So put your money where your mouth is and protect your darling husband."

Sam's mind raced. The idea of becoming Tyrell's property, of submitting to his control, was repulsive. But as much as she wanted to scream at him, to tell him where he could shove his twisted offer up his black ass, she knew she didn't have much of a choice. Mike's life was on the line, and Tyrell held all the power.

"Fine," she whispered, her voice breaking. "I'll do it. Just... just promise me you'll leave Mike alone."

"You have my word," Tyrell said smoothly, reaching out to caress her cheek. "Welcome to your new life, Sam."

CHAPTER SIX: Bound and Blindfolded

After promising herself to Tyrell, he wasted no time in showing her what he meant about making her his property. As soon as she told him that she would be his, he was leading her to his car, ready to whisk her away to his penthouse.

"Where are we going?" Sam asked, as he opened the door for her to make her way inside.

Tyrell got into the driver seat and started the car. He turned towards her and gave her a soft smile, the first of its kind since she started talking to him. "We are going to make good on our little arrangement, my dear."

Sam's heart pounded in her chest as she sat in the passenger seat of Tyrell's sleek black car. Tyrell suddenly reached over and took something out of the glove box in front of Sam.

"Put this on," Tyrell said, his voice commanding. He handed her a black silk blindfold. He locked eyes with her as if he was daring her to refuse.

Sam hesitated, staring at the blindfold in front of her. "Why do I need to wear this?" she asked.

Tyrell leaned closer, his breath warm against her ear. "Because I want you to. Do you really want to question me right now, Sam?"

The subtle threat had a dual effect on her, it sent a shiver of terror down her spine but it also gave her goosebumps, the kind that could only come from arousal. She knew she didn't have a choice in the matter but instead of making her feel completely helpless, she also felt strangely turned on.

With shaky hands, she tied the blindfold around her eyes, plunging herself into darkness.

The car started moving, and Sam's sense of direction was immediately thrown off thanks to the blindfold. The hum of the engine and the occasional bump in the road were the only indications that they were moving.

Finally, the car came to a stop. Sam heard the soft click of Tyrell's seatbelt, then the sound of his door opening and closing. A moment later, her door swung open, and Tyrell's hand gripped her arm firmly, guiding her out of the car.

"Careful now," he murmured, whispering against her ear as gently as his voice could go. His voice sounded smooth at this moment, was this because of the blindfold?

Tyrell kept her blindfolded as they walked, his hand never leaving her arm. Finally, they stopped and Sam could hear the creak of a door opening, followed by Tyrell gently pushing her forward.

No doubt they had entered a room, and she could smell the faint hint of lavender and something else that she couldn't quite place, it smelt similar to freshly washed silk.

Tyrell leaned closer and licked behind her ears with his tongue. "Don't take it off, your blindfold." Tyrell commanded as if reading her mind. "Not until I say so."

Sam nodded, her heart racing. She reached out her hands but there was nothing for her to grasp. He was completely in control of this situation and it made her feel incredibly vulnerable.

Tyrell suddenly put his hands on her shoulders, they were firm yes but they weren't harsh. It shook Sam as she did not expect any sort of gentility from Tyrell but she welcomed it. His touch was possessive and he slowly undressed her, letting each item of clothing fall to the floor.

The way he took the time to slip each item off her body, it was almost reverential. It made Sam feel honored, in a way she hadn't felt with Jay, Andre or even her husband.

"Do you trust me, Sam?" He asked against her ear as he dropped a kiss on her neck.

Sam scoffed. "Trust you? I don't exactly have the privilege to do that, do I?"

Tyrell chuckled loudly. "Good answer."

He slowly walked her over to the bed, his hands on her waist, trailing downwards till they cupped her ass. He smirked. "Damn, no way Mike's handling all that."

He pressed her down to the mattress and Sam could feel the silk sheets against her skin. Her body was tense, as it should be when it was in the presence of a man like Tyrell. She forced herself to relax, though; after all, the whole point of this was to submit to Tyrell's control.

Tyrell climbed in beside her, his hands roaming her body. Sam gasped when his hands cupped her breasts before he pinched her nipples between his fingers. Somehow the fact that she couldn't see only heightened her other senses so she felt everything. From the way he rolled her nipple between his fingers and the way his hand roamed all over her body.

"Right now Sam, you belong to me." He said, his breath hot against her skin. "I'm going to show you exactly what that means." His lips found her neck and he trailed hot kisses down to her collarbone then down past her navel to her vulva.

He finally settled himself between her thighs, causing her to shiver in anticipation. He parted her legs gently then she felt his warm breath against her skin.

His lips brushed her inner thighs and she gasped, bucking upwards in excitement. He took his time to explore her, pressing his tongue against her clit with pressure that gradually became firmer and more insistent.

His hands gripped her hips, holding her steady as his mouth worked wonders on her. She tangled her fingers into his hair when he began sucking on her clit lightly. She could feel herself getting overwhelmed and the pressure began to build within her.

His rhythm became more urgent and soon she had no choice but to cum right into his mouth. He didn't pull away immediately, instead let her ride her orgasm out. Only when she had come down from her high did he pull away, kiss up her body and then claim her lips. She could taste herself on him.

Tyrell moved quickly and before Sam knew what was happening, he had flipped her over and propped her up such that she was on her knees with her ass facing him, doggy-style.

She still couldn't see anything, she could only feel and she felt him use his dickhead to stroke her now very sensitive clitoris.

"I'm about to fuck the shit out of you." He said, groaning as he pushed himself into her. He grabbed her hips and gave a powerful thrust that made her cry out and hold onto the sheets. He filled her up completely and she could tell he was big from the way her pussy tingled as he made his way in.

He set a fast pace, driving into her without a care in a way that came off as possessive. Every thrust filled her with pleasure and she couldn't help but moan as he drove himself into her over and over again.

Her breath came out ragged as he moved inside her, the sound of his thighs slapping against her ass filled the room. His grip on her hips were firm and she could hear his own ragged breaths, clearly turned on by her body.

He leaned over her until she could feel his breath hot against her ear. "You feel so fucking good." he groaned, emphasizing his words with a several deep thrusts that sent waves of pleasure into her.

His hands slid up her spine and he reached for her hair, pulling her head back slightly. He angled his hips so his thrusts hit just the right spot over and over again. She could feel the tension in her body get tighter, meaning she was close.

But he was far from done with her.

CHAPTER SEVEN:
Unfinished Business

Tyrell was still buried deep inside of her. He kept his grip on her hips as he pulled out slowly, ever so slowly. It was like he was trying to tease her with the friction he was making. He gave her a small moment to catch her breath before he pulled her closer to him by her hips. He leaned over and whispered in her ear:

"On your back," he commanded, his voice low.

Sam knew that there was no point in resisting this man. So, turning over, Sam lay on her back. Tyrell wasted no time. He spread her legs wide, positioning himself between her thighs, and thrust back into her. The new angle sent shocks of pleasure through her, and her back arched off the bed as she moaned.

He set a slower, deliberate rhythm this time, pulling out nearly all the way before slamming back into her, making her toes curl.

"Fuck, Tyrell" she gasped, her nails digging into the sheets as her body writhed beneath him. He looked down at her intensely, he was enjoying watching her face contort from all the pleasure that he was giving her.

He leaned forward and took her lips into a harsh kiss, one that could leave a bruise if he pulled away. His hand slid between their bodies and found her clit, his fingers began to move in small circles around it. They worked in sync with his thrusts and the combination of the sensation was sending Sam over the edge.

Her body was shaking, she could feel herself getting closer. Tyrell could sense that she was getting close so he pulled back suddenly and flipped her onto her side.

Sam was taken aback by his sudden gesture and equally surprised by how nimble she was after all of these years. He was making her feel like a young woman again, the way he was flinging her around. He grabbed her legs and raised them as high as he could go as he positioned himself behind her.

This new position allowed him to drive even deeper into her, and Sam let out a loud moan as he pounded into her. His hand reached out and grabbed unto a tit, squeezing and pulling on her nipples as he buried himself to the hilt. The sound of skin slapping against skin grew louder in the room.

"You take me so fucking well," he groaned, "that's good."

Somehow his praise made Sam feel really good. If a man like this could tell her that she's good then maybe she was. He slammed into her relentlessly and Sam's head fell back.

She felt her orgasm building again but Tyrell wasn't slowing down. His pace quickened, his thrusts growing more erratic as he chased his release. Sam grew brazen and reached behind her, gripping his thigh, urging him. When he thrusted in one more time, her orgasm crashed over her like a tidal wave.

Her body clenched around him and her breath hitched as she came hard, her entire body shaking. Tyrell cursed under his breath and gripped her hips tighter as he gave four more deep thrusts then let out a long moan before pulling out and coming all over the place.

They stayed still for a moment, the sweat from their bodies falling onto the bed. Sam's chest heaved and her head was foggy from pleasure.

Tyrell stood up from the bed, still breathing hard, as he took his pants off his floor and began to get dressed. Sam remained in bed, unsure of what to do now.

"You're free to go," Tyrell said, his voice now cold once again. He glanced at her. "You did what you came here for."

Sam slowly got up from the bed, searching for her clothes, which were scattered all over the room. Tyrell didn't say anything else as she got dressed. He simply nodded towards the door, and she walked out of the room.

When she got out, she sat on the ground for a moment, her mind racing.

The guilt hit her first. She had done this for Mike, to save him from Tyrell and the life he had gotten tangled in. But even so, it felt wrong. This wasn't the same as her encounters with Andre or the others. Back then, it was consensual between her and Mike. He had known about it, had wanted it.

But this... this was different.

How had she gotten here? Her body still hummed with the lingering bliss of what had just happened. It scared her, how much she had enjoyed it. But she couldn't ignore the truth, it wasn't supposed to feel this good. Not like this, not with someone outside of the lifestyle she had entered with Mike's approval or someone who brought so much danger into their lives.

She stood up and started walking. She was doing this for her husband, she reminded herself, to free him from the hold Tyrell had over him. But even as she repeated that, it didn't feel justified.

By the time she got home, she found Mike in their bedroom. He asked her where she was coming from but she couldn't answer. She told him that she needed some rest and he let her be.

The next day, Mike woke up earlier than Sam then went to retrieve some mail. When he opened the door he found a package on his doorstep with a note attached. He looked around to see if anyone who had dropped it was close by. When he didn't see anybody, he brought it into the house.

He removed the note from the package and read it, his blood running cold as. he did so.

"Heard you liked watching your wife fuck big black men. Watch this."

Frantically, he opened the package and in it he found a USB. Rushing to his bedroom and trying not to wake Sam up, he inserted the USB into their computer and to his shock, it was a video of Tyrell taking his wife from behind.

Mike stood there, completely taken aback at what he was seeing. What was this about? When did this happen? He thought to himself.

"Mike," He heard a voice behind him say. He turned around to see his wife looking at him with guilt. "Mike, I can explain."

What explanation could she possibly give that would justify her sleeping with the man that was ruining his life?

THE END OF BOOK THREE

Dear reader,

Thank you for reading to the end! I hope the book lived up to your expectations!

Would you like to read part four? Part four is the final part in this series! It's available at Amazon as well; just go to this book's product page or series page!

Exclusive erotic short story club
Want even more? You can join my exclusive erotic short club **for free**. By doing so, you will get a bunch of free stories (before I publish them on Amazon), audiobook coupon codes, and much more! Join here: https://bit.ly/3WJsqRp

Or email me at amber.carden.books@gmail.com and I will send you a link!

Amber

© Copyright 2024 - All rights reserved.

The content contained within this book may not be reproduced, duplicated, or transmitted without direct written permission from the author or the publisher.

This book is copyright protected. It is only for personal use. You cannot amend, distribute, sell, use, quote or paraphrase any part, or the content within this book, without the consent of the author or publisher.

www.ingramcontent.com/pod-product-compliance
Lightning Source LLC
LaVergne TN
LVHW041634070526
838199LV00052B/3348